written by
EMMA WUNSCH

illustrated by
JESSIKA VON INNEREBNER

Amulet Books
New York

Miranda AND MAUDE ②

BANANA PANTS!

BY EMMA WUNSCH ☙ ILLUSTRATED BY JESSIKA VON INNEREBNER

For anyone who's ever had to say sorry

Library of Congress Cataloging-in-Publication Data
Names: Wunsch, Emma, author. | Von Innerebner, Jessika, illustrator.
Title: Banana pants! / Emma Wunsch; illustrated by Jessika von Innerebner.
Description: New York: Amulet Books, 2019. | Series: Miranda and Maude ; volume 2 | Summary: Fed-up with standardized testing, Miranda and Maude's teacher decides to put on a school play, inspiring the girls to fight for other positive changes—and leading to their first fight.
Identifiers: LCCN 2018024296 (print) | LCCN 2018030104 (ebook) | ISBN 9781683354772 (All e-books) | ISBN 9781419731808 (hardcover pob)
Subjects: | CYAC: Schools—Fiction. | Theater—Fiction. | Princesses—Fiction. | Social action—Fiction. | Friendship—Fiction. Classification: LCC PZ7.1.W97 (ebook) | LCC PZ7.1.W97 Ban 2019 (print) | DDC [E]—dc23

ABRAMS The Art of Books
195 Broadway, New York, NY 10007
abramsbooks.com

THE
Miranda
AND
MAUDE
SERIES

1

EXTRA–EXTRA EARLY MONDAY MORNING

One Monday morning, Princess Miranda Rose Lapointsetta went into her classroom, 3B, at Mountain River Valley Elementary extra-extra early. She was there for extra-extra help from her favorite teacher, Miss Kinde.

Before this year, Miranda had never been to school. She was a princess who lived in a castle and had a very old tutor who didn't teach her much. When Madame Cornelia retired, Miranda's parents (Queen Mom and King Dad, or QM and KD for short) made her go to school. At first, school was terrible. It smelled like hard-boiled eggs, everything was loud and confusing, and she always had a headache. Worst of all, she had no friends.

But then a bunch of things happened, and Miranda became best friends with Maude

Brandywine Mayhew Kaye, who was absolutely not a princess. Once Miranda had a friend and learned she needed glasses, she began to enjoy school. Things she once hated, like music class (which was very loud), lunch (which was very smelly), and PE (which was a little bit dangerous) were now practically okay, because everything was better when you had a friend to agree with you about how loud, smelly, and dangerous things were.

But right now, Miranda's classroom was not loud or smelly or dangerous. 3B was quiet, because she was the only student there, and it smelled like lavender, because that was what Miranda's beloved teacher, Miss Kinde, smelled like. Miss Kinde was just like her name. Kind! Wonderful! Amazing! She was always interested in what Miranda had to say and, best of all, even though she often reminded Miranda and Maude to stop talking to each other, she never switched their seats!

The only bad thing about Miss Kinde's class, Miranda thought that early Monday morning, *isn't about Miss Kinde at all*. It was about a test.

A famously awful test called the Mandatory National Reading and Writing and Math Exam, which every student had to take at the end of the school year. Since the beginning of the year (which wasn't that long ago), Miss Kinde had given 3B many, many practice exams. Because Miranda had never taken the exam before, and since Principal Fish thought it was extremely

important, she often had to spend her extra extra help time taking practice tests.

"I'm sorry to give you another exam," Miss Kinde said sadly, handing Miranda a thick booklet.

"It's not your fault," Miranda said unhappily. Not only were the practice exams long, they were also confusing and boring. The exams caused fear and misery in both students and teachers alike. They took up time from the things the students and teachers really wanted to do.

Sighing, Miranda looked at the clock, grabbed a pencil from Maude's desk, and waited for Miss Kinde to tell her to begin.

But before Miss Kinde could say "begin," Maude Brandywine Mayhew Kaye roller-skated into the classroom yelling, "HELP!"

MAUDE BRANDYWINE MAYHEW KAYE TRULY NEEDS HELP

Miss Kinde and Miranda stood up. Did Maude need help stopping? But Maude came to an easy stop, plunked down on Miranda's desk, and took off her skates.

"What are you doing here?" Miranda asked. She was shocked to see her best friend, who often slept through her alarm clock (a crowing rooster named General Cockatoo) and always arrived almost-late to school.

"I saw the sunrise over Mount Coffee!" Maude said excitedly.

"That's wonderful," Miss Kinde said. "And it's wonderful to see you, Maude, but you do remember rules forty-six and fifty-eight?"

Rule forty-six in the *Official Rules of Mountain River Valley Elementary* said that students were not allowed in school until 7:42 a.m. unless they were getting help. Rule fifty-eight said that wheeled shoes were forbidden in school.

"I know *all* the rules," Maude said. "And I truly need help!"

Miss Kinde smiled at Maude, who was wearing paint-splattered pants, a wrinkled T-shirt that said SAVE THE HUMPHEAD WRASSE, and a pair of glasses that she loved but didn't need.

"I don't think you need help," Miss Kinde said

patiently. "You did tremendously well on Friday's practice exam."

"Did I beat Hillary?" Maude asked. She moved her glasses onto the top of her head.

Hillary was Hillary Greenlight-Miller, Maude's archenemy and the only person in 3B (or maybe the world) who did not dread practice exams.

Miss Kinde did not answer Maude's question.

"Never mind," Maude said. "It's not important! What's important are these!" She took a stack of letters out of her messenger bag. "Everyone keeps saying no!" Maude cried. "I write letter after letter demanding change and nothing ever happens."

"What kind of change?" Miss Kinde asked gently.

"Change for good!" Maude held out a letter. "Except no one will change! I wrote to Chemical Apple to say that they should stop putting chemicals on their apples. Do you know what they wrote back?"

Miss Kinde and Miranda shook their heads. Maude read:

Dear Maude Brandywine Mayhew Kaye,

Thank you for yet another letter suggesting Chemical Apple Inc. stop using chemicals on our apple trees. Unfortunately, at this time, that is impossible.

Sincerely,

E. Vole Mann McGoo
President, Chemical Apple Inc.

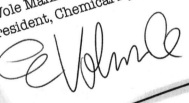

"Oh dear." Miss Kinde cleared her throat and looked at the clock. They were dangerously close to running out of time for Miranda's exam.

"*Impossible?!*" Maude bellowed. "It's *not* impossible! When you do something wrong, you apologize. You say, 'Sorry, that was a terrible idea. I won't do it ever again'!"

Miss Kinde nodded, but Miranda yawned. She couldn't help it. Maude was her absolutely positively best friend, but not everything that interested Maude interested her. Some things, like whatever Maude was talking about right now, really bored her.

Maude had her hand in a fist and was talking quickly to Miss Kinde. "I did exactly what you told me, Miss Kinde. I said what the problem was and explained why it's bad. But every letter I get back says the same thing! 'We're going to keep fishing,' 'We're going to keep poisoning apples,' 'We can't clean the lake,' 'Styrofoam forever'!"

"Styrofoam?" Miss Kinde asked.

"Principal Fish," Maude groaned. "No matter

how many times I tell him that Styrofoam is terrible, he won't do anything about the lunch trays."

Miss Kinde coughed a little. "Maude, it's inspiring to see how much you care about world issues. I am impressed with your many good causes, and I know how disappointed you must be."

"I am *terribly* disappointed. What should I do, Miss Kinde? I need help," Maude begged.

Miss Kinde hesitated and then said, "Well, maybe some of your classmates could write letters, too. Sometimes it helps if there's more than

one voice." She glanced at Miranda, who seemed to be falling asleep.

Maude looked at Miranda. "I could write so many more letters if you wrote letters, too!"

Miranda yawned again and shook her head. There was no way she was writing letters! "I'm really busy," she told Maude, pointing to the practice exam on her desk.

"Too busy to save the world?" Maude asked. "Too busy for peace and justice and a clean earth?"

But you're not actually saving the world, Miranda thought, looking at the pile of Maude's letters. *You're probably just giving yourself a hand cramp and wasting ink.*

"What do you care about?" Maude asked Miranda. "You must care about something."

"I care about lots of things," Miranda said quietly. "But letter writing is not one of them."

The girls looked at each other. Even though they were extremely different, they always got along. And now it wasn't that they were fighting exactly. But no matter how much Maude wanted her to, Miranda just couldn't care about letter writing.

No one said anything. Miss Kinde sneezed, and Miranda and Maude both handed her a tissue. Miss Kinde blew her nose and looked at the clock.

And then Walter Matthews Mayhew Kaye the eighth walked into 3B.

3

ABSOLUTELY, POSITIVELY SWIMMING IN SOUP

"Dad?" Maude said. "What are you doing here?"

"You left so early, my beautiful bark beetle, you forgot your lunch!" He handed her a metal container and a large spoon.

"No beetle names in school, Dad," Maude

whispered. "And I didn't forget it, I *left* it. On purpose. I'm sick of soup."

"It smells delicious," Miss Kinde said. "At least I think it does. I believe I'm getting a cold."

"Take it," Maude grumbled. "I've had soup for breakfast, lunch, and dinner and breakfast, lunch, and dinner!"

"I can't eat your soup, Maude." Miss Kinde suddenly sounded congested.

"Please! I beg you, Miss Kinde. We're swimming in it."

Miranda laughed, thinking about how much soup she'd helped Maude and her family make over the weekend. She might not like letter writing, but spending time at Maude's house was one of her favorite things to do.

You never knew what fun you might have over at Maude's, which was a houseboat in the trees. Maude's brother, Michael-John, might teach you a very unusual word (this weekend's word was *hircine*), or her dad might recite quotes and interesting facts about beetles. You might dance with Onion the Great Number Eleven (a cat), or bathe

Rudolph Valentino (a dog), or give a shower to Rosalie (a chicken)! You might help build a classic car and then get driven all over town! Or you might make gallons upon gallons of soup.

"Let's trade," Maude suggested to Miss Kinde. "What do you have for lunch?"

Miss Kinde turned pink. "Well, um . . ." she said. "Actually, I have soup. But it's not homemade. I bought it at the store."

"Oh dear," Walt said. "Well, then you must take Maude's! Homemade soup is so much better! No matter how busy I am, I always try to find time to make soup."

"But . . ." Miss Kinde sputtered.

"Maude can share mine," Miranda told her. "Chef Blue always packs enormous lunches."

"Great idea," Maude said.

Miranda hoped a non-soup lunch would stop Maude from asking her to write a billion boring letters.

Miss Kinde took the container, unscrewed the lid, and inhaled. "Mmm . . ." she said. "But students can't share food."

"Who cares about rules twelve and thirteen?" Maude said. "They're just words."

"Speaking of words," Walt said, "the French playwright Molière said, 'I live on good soup, not on fine words.' Isn't that lovely?"

Miss Kinde beamed. "I love plays!"

Walt grinned. "There's nothing like theater, is there?"

Listening to Miss Kinde and Walt talk about soup and theater gave Miranda a warm and happy feeling.

"Dad," Maude said, "don't you have to go discover a beetle or something?"

Walt looked at the clock and jumped. "Indeed, I do. I'm off to an important beetle conference, where I'm going to share my latest beetle discovery!"

"Wow!" Miss Kinde sounded impressed.

"I apologize for the interruption," Walt said.

"Quite all right," Miss Kinde said. "Thanks for the soup."

After Walt left, Miss Kinde put Miranda's unanswered practice exam back on her desk. "Since there's not enough time for the test, I'll just put this wonderful soup in the teachers' lounge," she said, stepping out into the hall.

Once their teacher was gone, Miranda turned to Maude. "I know what I care about," she said.

"Hooray," Maude said. "I couldn't have a best

friend who didn't care about something. What's your cause? Saving the pangolins? Cleaning Lemon Lake? Getting rid of the Styrofoam lunch trays?"

"Love," Miranda said.

Maude stared at her friend. "Love? What does love have to do with changing the world?"

"A lot."

"Boyfriends and girlfriends and dumb dates and stupid kissing has nothing to do with changing the world!"

"I mean love like being happy," Miranda said. "Your dad and Miss Kinde looked happy talking to each other about soup and plays!" She smiled. "Maybe they could go to a play. And eat soup afterward. They both love soup and plays!"

"That's ridiculous." Maude grimaced.

"Why?" Miranda asked. "Miss Kinde needs homemade soup, especially with her cold, and your dad needs friends. Just this weekend he said he wished there were more people over to enjoy all the soup we made."

Maude didn't remember her father saying

that. *Had he?* Between the soup making and her letter writing and hanging out with her beloved animals and Miranda, Maude hadn't heard. But still. Love was not a cause! "My dad is too busy for friends," she told Miranda. "He's got me, Michael-John, his beetles, his yoga, and his quotes."

"No one is too busy for friends," Miranda said.

"Well, my dad is!"

Miranda didn't say anything.

"Don't get my dad into any love cause or anything. Okay?"

"Okay," Miranda said quietly as the morning bell rang and Miss Kinde came back in.

4

A RULE-BREAKING ANNOUNCEMENT

When everyone in 3B was at their desks, Miss Kinde asked, as she did every Monday, how their weekends had been.

"Awesome!" Norris told her. "I played pickleball and got a lava lamp!"

"I made French crullers," Donut said. "They weren't perfect, but they were delicious."

"My weekend was great," Agnes said. "Agatha slept over. We stayed up really late sewing tiny clothes for tiny animals."

"I was in a gymnastics show," Desdemona announced proudly.

"I came up with an amazing title for a new science fiction story I'm going to write," Norbert said. *"Avenging Alien Bees!"*

"My stepmom taught me how to dance the jitterbug," Fletcher said.

"I built the Eiffel Tower!" Felix grinned proudly. "I used three gallons of glue and two thousand and nine popsicle sticks."

"My weekend, as you already know, was soupy," Maude said. "Me, my dad, my brother, and Miranda made nine million gallons of soup," she

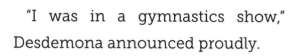

told the class. "I also had some unfortunate correspondence from some evil corporations, but I'm hoping my best friend will help me change that." She looked at Miranda. Miranda stared at her hands. Her hands did not want to write letters to evil corporations. Her hands did not want to write any letters at all.

"You didn't make nine million gallons of soup," Hillary Greenlight-Miller informed Maude.

"I did."

"Impossible," Hillary said.

"How was *your* weekend, Hillary?" Miss Kinde asked, to change the subject.

"Productive," Hillary told her. "I went over eight practice exams and read the next five chapters in the science book."

The class groaned. *Why would Hillary do practice exams and read her science book over the weekend?*

Miss Kinde sniffled. "I hope you had fun, too, Hillary. Weekends should be a break from schoolwork."

"Did you have a nice weekend, Miss Kinde?"

Miranda asked, suddenly curious about what her teacher did when she wasn't at school.

Miss Kinde looked surprised, but sounded pleased when she said, "Thanks for asking, Miranda. My weekend was—"

"What did you do?" Norris asked.

"Did you bake?" Donut asked.

"Sew?"

"Glue?"

"Do a one-handed cartwheel?"

"Well," Miss Kinde said, "I, um, to be honest, class, I graded practice exams."

"The whole weekend?" Maude asked, horrified.

Miss Kinde shrugged. "There are sixteen of you. You take seven or eight exams a week. That's . . ."

"One hundred twenty-eight exams!" Maude yelled.

"One hundred twelve exams!" Hillary Greenlight-Miller shouted.

"It's a lot to grade," Miss Kinde said quietly. "It takes time."

The class nodded. Poor Miss Kinde!

"And speaking of time," Miss Kinde said. "It's time to start today's exam." She handed out green papers. "Take one and pass the rest," she said robotically.

Donut raised his hand. "Miss Kinde? How many more practice exams do we have to take? Before we take the real one."

Miss Kinde looked at Donut. Then she looked at the rest of her class. She was quiet for so long that Hillary Greenlight-Miller began frantically waving her hands. "Miss Kinde!" she said. "Miss Kinde!"

Miss Kinde blinked and came back to 3B. "One hundred and ninety-two," she told Donut. "At the very least."

"One hundred ninety-two more practice exams for each of us?" Donut said in horror.

Miss Kinde looked at her students. "Class," she said, "give me back your practice exams."

"But we haven't done them!" Hillary screeched.

"I know," Miss Kinde said calmly. "I know you haven't done them, Hillary. But we've done so many, and sometimes, I think Mountain River Valley Elementary spends too much time on tests and not enough time on . . ."

"Fun stuff!" Maude shouted. "We take so many tests we don't have enough time for . . . fun stuff!" She held up her fist, even though she wished she had a more chant-worthy phrase than "fun stuff."

Miss Kinde nodded. She stacked all of the unanswered practice exams back on her desk.

3B looked at Miss Kinde. Miss Kinde looked at 3B. The classroom was very quiet, and not in a test-taking way. It was quiet in a what's-going-to-happen-next way.

"Now what?" Hillary asked.

Miss Kinde shrugged.

Hillary's eyes bulged.

Miss Kinde looked at her students. "Real

learning," she said, "isn't just doing a million practice exams. Real learning is about love."

Yes, Miranda thought, sitting up a little taller. Love *was* important. Her teacher said so!

"Love?" Norbert groaned. "Love is gross."

"I want you to feel excited about something," Miss Kinde explained. "Love what you do." She looked at Maude. "Even when it's hard. Especially when it's hard and maybe doesn't go the way you want. Who here feels passionate about practice exams?"

Hillary Greenlight-Miller almost raised her hand. But then she decided what she actually loved was being the first to finish and getting higher scores than Maude.

"But we need to do *something*," Hillary insisted. "Our school day is really long."

"Today, I want you to do something that you care about," Miss Kinde said. "Do something that brings you joy, even if it's not easy."

The class looked at one another. *Joy?* they wondered. *In school?*

"I care!" Maude shouted. "I care about all my

very important causes!" She looked at Miranda. "If I don't have to take a test, I'll write the best letter I've ever written!" *And maybe Miranda will write one, too*, she thought.

"I care about what will happen when aveng- ing alien bees break out of the lab," Norbert said. "Maybe I could work on my story?"

"Excellent," Miss Kinde said.

"I care about doughnuts," Donut said. "With all this free time, I'll go to the doughnut shop!" He grinned. "I'll get enough for the whole class. You, too, Miss Kinde."

"You can't leave school," Miss Kinde informed Donut. "But we won't take any practice exams. Today will be for creative endeavors!"

"What's *endeavors*?" Miranda and Donut asked. They looked at Maude, but it was Hillary who said, "An endeavor is a work with a set purpose."

Miss Kinde nodded. "Today will be Three B's creative endeavor day!"

"Hooray!" the class cheered.

"Of course, first I must talk to Principal Fish," Miss Kinde said quickly.

3B groaned. Rule-loving Principal Fish would never let them skip a practice exam for a creative endeavor. Even if *endeavor* was one of the

vocabulary words on today's exam. But Miss Kinde cleared her throat, blew her nose, straightened her spine, and held her head high. "I'll be back," she said, slipping into the hall.

5

PRACTICE EXAM EIGHT MILLION AND THREE

3B was unusually silent while their teacher was gone. Maude thought about all the letters she'd be able to write if Miss Kinde convinced Principal Fish that they shouldn't take a test. She looked at Miranda, who was staring into space. *There has to be a way to get Miranda to write a letter*, she thought.

Miranda was picturing Walt and Miss Kinde sharing soup, talking about theater, and reciting quotes. *How can that happen?* she wondered.

When Miss Kinde came back, her nose was running and she was a little out of breath. She inhaled deeply and said, "Class, if you learn anything this year, I'd like you to learn that sometimes ideas need to happen before others can see how good they are."

"Hear, hear," Maude muttered, looking at the letters in her bag.

Yes, Miranda thought. Once Maude saw how happy her dad and Miss Kinde were together, she'd realize Miranda had been right. Love was an extremely important cause!

"Principal Fish has agreed that for the next two weeks, Three B will not take any practice exams."

"Hooray!" 3B shouted, not believing their good fortune. Two whole weeks without tests! That was amazing! That was incredible! That was—

"But . . ." Miss Kinde paused. "Principal Fish wants us to do or make something as a class."

"All together?" 3B asked all together.

Miss Kinde nodded and sneezed. "And we need to show the whole school what we've done."

"Let's write letters!" Maude stood up. "We could write a gazillion letters in two weeks!"

"No," 3B said.

"Let's have a rally then," Maude said. "We'll make posters and buttons and start a petition!"

"No," 3B said again.

"Don't you guys want buttons?" Maude asked quietly.

"What are we rallying for?" Donut asked, pulling the thread of a small hole in his pants.

"We can rally for whatever we want. Or whatever we *don't* want. Chemical Apple, Fishmann Fisheries. Speaking of fish, how about a rally against Principal Fish for using Styrofoam trays."

"That's just stuff *you* want to do, Maude," Hillary said. "No one else does. You don't even eat school lunch."

Maude sat back down. "Do you have a better idea?"

"No," Hillary mumbled.

"We could bake something huge," Donut suggested.

"Count me out," Norbert told him. "I almost killed my family by using rotten eggs once. We vomited for days!"

"Let's build an Eiffel Tower out of two-by-fours," Felix said.

"We can't fit an Eiffel Tower in our classroom," Agatha told him.

"There's no endeavor we can do together," Hillary informed Miss Kinde.

"Think!" Maude yelled. "If we don't come up with anything, we're going to have to take practice exam number eight million and three."

For a second it looked like Hillary was going to correct Maude on her math, but she said nothing.

While the class desperately thought of something they could do together, Fletcher tapped his feet, Donut pulled harder at the now medium-size hole in his pants, and Miranda cleaned her glasses and put them back on.

Even though she'd had glasses for a while, Miranda was still amazed by how much better the world looked now that she could really see. She looked around the room for inspiration. Another reason why she loved Miss Kinde was because even though it broke a lot of rules, her teacher let her bring things from the castle to improve the classroom. Thanks to Miranda, 3B now had

beanbag chairs, fluffy rugs, striped pillows, and yellow curtains.

The curtains are a nice touch, Miranda thought. *They are much nicer than the curtain hanging in the auditorium.*

Auditorium . . . Miranda thought. There was a stage in the auditorium. A stage that could be used for a play! Miss Kinde and Walt both liked plays. If 3B endeavored to put on a play, then Walt and Miss Kinde could watch it together! And have soup when it was over.

"A play!" Miranda shrieked.

3B stared at her. She'd never shrieked before.

"We could do a class play," she explained in

her usual quiet voice. "Felix could build the sets, since he likes to glue. Agnes and Agatha could make costumes, since they like to sew."

Felix, Agnes, and Agatha all nodded.

"I could do the dances," Fletcher offered. "I'd be the . . . choreographer?" He looked at Miss Kinde, who nodded.

"Craft services," Donut said, excitedly pulling on the getting-much-bigger hole in his pants.

3B looked at him.

"Snacks," Donut explained. "I'll bring food to the rehearsals."

"I'll direct," Hillary and Maude announced.

"I can write it," Norbert offered. "I've always wanted to write a play."

Miranda looked around the classroom, wondering what she could do. She didn't want to direct or write, and she wasn't great at sewing or gluing. Too bad there wasn't anything that involved lamps or curtains.

Miranda must have looked unsure, because Miss Kinde looked at her and said, "Miranda, you could be the prop master! A prop master sets the scene. You'll be excellent, since you have such terrific taste when it comes to curtains, lamps, and where things should be placed."

3B looked around their improved classroom and nodded.

"Prop master," Miranda said to Maude. "I like the sound of that."

"I'll direct," Hillary and Maude said again.

"What are we calling our play?" Norbert asked. "I can't start writing without a title."

3B looked at one another. What *should* their play be called? Fletcher began tapping his feet again. Desdemona scratched a bug bite on her hand. Norbert pulled on his sweatshirt hood and slunk down in his seat. Maude reached into her bag, past the stack of letters, roller skates, a rusty harmonica, and a curly chicken feather. She was looking for her lucky letter-writing pen to write down all the reasons she'd make a better director than Hillary, but to her surprise, she took out an overripe, extremely smelly banana instead.

At that very moment, overwhelmed by the

strong banana smell, Donut pulled the string on his pants so hard that his pant leg split completely down the middle.

"What a banana!" Maude said in amazement.

"My pants!" Donut cried.

Miranda, holding her nose, looked at Maude's banana and Donut's pants. And then she said, very dramatically, *Banana Pants*! Our play should be called *Banana Pants*!"

6

A SCAD OF SCAD SOUP

"School was amazing today!" Maude told her dad and brother when she got home that Monday afternoon. Walt was stirring soup on the stove. Michael-John was on the couch, reading the definition of the word *vainglorious*, which is an adjective meaning boastful.

"Miss Kinde cares so much about Three B that she stood up to Principal Fish!" Maude kissed Rudolph Valentino, patted Onion the Great Number Eleven between her ears, and picked up her Frizzle chicken, Rosalie, and spun her around.

"She seems like a lovely person," Walt said quietly.

Maude stopped spinning and made a face. "Lovely" was a little too close to "love" for her. *Who needs all this stupid love stuff?* "Anyway, because Miss Kinde stood up for our rights, Three B isn't going to have any practice exams for two whole weeks!"

"Sounds wonderful." Walt spooned soup into a bowl. "I'm glad *your* day was good, Maude. Mine was terribly disappointing."

"We're going to do a creative endeavor! A play. I'll probably be the director!"

"The great William Shakespeare said, 'All the world's a stage,'" Walt said. "Eat some soup, Maude. There's so much left."

Maude put her chicken on the table and sat down. "Our play is called *Banana Pants*. It's going to be about a kid who finds some pants. That's all we know so far. Norbert hasn't decided if the pants will be good or evil yet."

Walt sighed.

"I think they'll be yellow," Maude crooned to Rosalie.

Walt sighed again, deeply.

"Why was your day so rotten?" Maude finally asked.

"Unfortunately, at today's conference, I discovered that my latest beetle discovery had already been discovered."

"Bummer," said Maude.

"I was so close . . . and yet so very far away."

"Do I have to have soup?" Maude asked. "How much is left?"

"A scad," Michael-John called from the couch. "*Scad* is a noun. It means a large quantity."

"Ugh," Maude said.

"Scad can also be a kind of fish," Michael-John added. "We should be happy that Dad didn't make a scad of scad soup. Eat some, Maude. I ate six bowls today and didn't make a dent."

"I'm so tired of soup. Can I have a hard-boiled egg?" Before Maude was best friends with Miranda, she'd eaten hard-boiled eggs all the time. But once she learned how much Miranda hated them, she'd stopped bringing them to school.

"We don't have any," Walt said. "Since Miranda is so sensitive to the smell."

"But she's not here. She can't smell an egg in a castle that's one point two miles away."

"Yes, but she's here so often, I've stopped making them," Walt said.

"A mighty powerful princess," Michael-John said. "To keep you away from your hard-boiled eggs."

Maude tried to remember how many hard-boiled eggs she'd eaten since she and Miranda had become best friends. *Not one!* Maybe Miranda had more power than Maude realized. She was a princess, after all.

So why can't she write just one letter?

Chemical Apple or Principal Fish would notice a letter from a princess! And maybe they would finally do something. Miss Kinde was right. It was important that evil corporations hear from other people, not just from Maude. An idea began to form in Maude's brain. She pushed Rosalie out of the way and tore a clean page out of her notebook.

"Maude?" Walt asked. "Your soup is getting cold."

But Maude didn't answer. She was writing another letter.

7

HUMBLY, FERDINAND F. FISH

Maude worked on her letter for most of the afternoon. She took a break to eat dinner (more soup) and then took the letter to her room to read it to Rosalie, who was pecking at something on the bed.

Dear Principal Fish,

I am writing because Mountain River Valley should stop using Styrofoam lunch trays in the cafeteria. Styrofoam is bad! It hurts the environment. Pieces of Styrofoam get into the oceans and make sea life sick. Styrofoam is also bad because it can stick to the food that students eat. That is gross! I beg you to stop using Styrofoam trays and to use recyclable ones instead. Then Mountain River Valley wouldn't have so much garbage. Too much garbage is also a problem, but I will not write about that in this letter.

Sincerely . . .

"It's a very good letter," Maude told her chicken. Rosalie clucked.

"But it sounds like all the other letters I've written to Principal Fish."

Rosalie sat down on Maude's pillow.

"If I write 'Sincerely, Maude Brandywine Mayhew Kaye,' Principal Fish will just throw this letter in the garbage. He probably doesn't even recycle." Maude stood up and put on her glasses.

"Principal Fish would notice a letter from Miranda, because he never gets letters from princesses."

Maude imagined Miranda receiving a letter from Principal Fish that read:

> *Dear Miranda,*
>
> *Thank you for the well-written and excellently spelled letter. Mountain River Valley will never use Styrofoam again!*
>
> *Humbly,*
>
> *Ferdinand F. Fish*
>
> *Principal, Mountain River Valley Elementary*

Miranda would like a letter like that, Maude thought. *She probably won't mind if I sign her name just one little time.* Maude picked up her lucky letter-writing pen. And with that, Maude signed the letter on her desk:

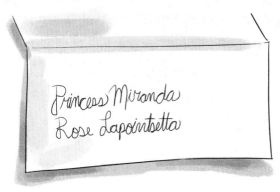

8

MAUDE DELIVERS THE LETTER

Very early Tuesday morning, Maude, who was not wearing roller skates, crept down the hall of Mountain River Valley Elementary.

Despite her soft walking, Principal Fish stopped her outside the library. "ARE YOU HERE FOR EXTRA-EXTRA HELP?" he bellowed.

"No," Maude said. "But I need another copy of the *Official Rules of Mountain River Valley Elementary*. My Frizzle chicken ate mine."

Principal Fish twirled his long mustache between his fingers.

"I don't believe," Maude said quickly, "that getting another rule book breaks any rules." Maude actually knew it was not against the rules, because she'd double-checked her perfectly fine, non-eaten rule book the night before.

Principal Fish tapped his index finger on his temple and boomed, "FOLLOW ME!"

Maude followed Principal Fish into his office. When he turned to get a rule book from a high shelf, Maude put the princess-signed letter right in the middle of his desk.

Principal Fish handed Maude the rule book she didn't want or need. "KEEP THIS AWAY FROM THE CHICKEN," he commanded.

"I will," Maude said. And then, even though it broke several rules, she skipped out of his office and ran all the way down the hall.

9

THE MOST UNUSUAL WEDNESDAY IN THE HISTORY OF MOUNTAIN RIVER VALLEY ELEMENTARY

The next day was quite possibly the most unusual Wednesday in the history of Mountain River Valley Elementary.

The first unusual thing was that Miss Kinde took a sick day. Since she'd never before been absent, 3B was confused when the last bell rang and their teacher wasn't there.

And then Principal Fish walked in. "MISS KINDE IS ILL," he thundered. "AND NO SUBSTITUTES ARE AVAILABLE. RULE SIXTY-TWO SAYS THAT IF NO SUBSTITUTE IS AVAILABLE, THE PRINCIPAL MUST FILL IN. AS PRINCIPAL, I MUST FILL IN."

3B groaned silently. They would have

groaned out loud, but they didn't want to break rule eighty-five with Principal Fish right there.

"Can we still work on our creative endeavor?" Norbert asked, picking up a long yellow pad of paper.

Principal Fish said nothing.

"I thought of some excellent dance moves," Fletcher said. "I can teach them to everyone if we move our desks out of the way."

"Then we can do our handsprings,"Desdemona added eagerly.

"We brought our tape measures," Agatha and Agnes said. "We'll take measurements so we can work on the pants."

"THERE WILL BE NO DANCE MOVES," Principal Fish bellowed. "THERE WILL BE NO HANDSPRINGS! THERE WILL BE NO PANTS! THERE WILL BE A PRACTICE EXAM."

3B sighed sadly. Without Miss Kinde, they wouldn't get to work on their creative endeavor.

But actually, there was no practice exam. Principal Fish couldn't find the key to the file cabinet where all the exams were kept. Principal Fish, very unhappy about not being able to give the exam, ordered the class to do something quietly while he searched for the key.

Silently, 3B took the opportunity to work on *Banana Pants*. Agnes and Agatha passed around their tape measures so everyone in the class could secretly measure. Fletcher showed Desdemona and Felix his dance ideas with his fingers. Norbert put his yellow pad on the far-right side of his desk so that Norris could read what he was writing. After Felix watched

Fletcher's fingers dance, he sketched a few sets and showed them to Miranda, who tried to think of matching props. Silently, Maude and Hillary each wrote a lengthy list of reasons why she should be director.

And then, just when Norbert was getting to the big action scene, Principal Fish boomed that he'd found the key (which was on the hook marked KEY HOOK next to the cabinet).

The day turned more usual after that. Principal Fish gave 3B a practice exam and then escorted them to lunch.

It was during lunch that the most unusual thing happened.

"Look! Look at my lunch!" Donut hollered.

Maude stopped slurping soup and Miranda stopped nibbling cheese. They looked at Donut's lunch, but to them it looked like all school lunches: gray and lumpy.

"It just looks gross," Maude said. "Sorry, Donut."

"Don't look at the food. Look at the tray!"

Maude's eyes practically doubled in size. The tray was plastic! A lovely, recyclable plastic. She reached out and touched Donut's lunch tray.

"It's not Styrofoam!" Maude shouted, jumping up. "It worked! It worked! It worked!"

"What worked?" Donut asked.

"The—" Maude looked at Miranda. Was it the letter she'd written for Miranda? Was *that* the letter that finally worked? Maude opened her mouth but said nothing.

"Principal Fish finally answered your letters," Miranda said.

Maude nodded.

"And you didn't even need me," Miranda said happily.

Maude looked at Miranda, then back at Donut's tray. "I guess I didn't," she said.

10

A MUCH MORE USUAL THURSDAY

Everything was mostly back to normal on Thursday. Miss Kinde returned with only a slight sniffle, so 3B got to work on their creative endeavor as loudly as they wanted. Felix and Miranda talked about sets and prop locations while Fletcher and Desdemona practiced their pliés and handsprings. Norris, reading over Norbert's shoulder, offered synonyms for words like *tremendous* and *exceptional*. Other than the unusualness of having so much fun in school, the only unusual thing that happened was at lunch, when Maude announced that Hillary Greenlight-Miller could direct *Banana Pants*.

Hillary nearly choked

mid-swallow. Once she recovered, she was, for once, speechless.

"Really?" Miranda asked Maude. She'd never known Maude to back down so easily. Especially not with Hillary.

Maude nodded. "I'm too busy."

"With what?" Miranda asked.

"My chickens, my tomatoes, stuff like that," Maude said quickly.

"But it's not tomato season. And I thought Rosalie was happy now that she's officially the house chicken."

"Well . . ." Maude looked at the rows of recyclable lunch trays that lined their table. "I have improved my method of letter writing," she said. "And it might be working. I should focus on that."

"That's great!" Miranda felt happy that Maude was happy and was also extremely relieved that it didn't require her to write a single word.

11

MIRANDA'S EAST LIBRARY DISCOVERY

When Miranda got home from school that usual Thursday, she stopped for a quick snack with her parents.

"How's *Apple Skirt* going?" KD asked.

"*Banana Pants*," Miranda corrected. "Our play is called *Banana Pants*. I'm the prop master. Miss Kinde said I have a wonderful eye."

"And not just because of your new glasses." KD chuckled.

"Sounds exciting," QM said.

"It is," Miranda said. And the play would be even more exciting if Miranda could use it to show Maude how happy Walt and Miss Kinde would be together! Then Maude would agree that love was an important cause.

But how could she get this to happen? She looked up at the chandelier, but the only idea she

got was that it would make an excellent prop for *Banana Pants*.

"Can I bring the chandelier to school?" Miranda asked.

"Absolutely not," QM said. "It's screwed into the ceiling!"

"But feel free to use anything that isn't nailed down," KD said.

QM gave KD a look, but he missed it.

"Great," Miranda said. "I'll go look for props right now."

Miranda wandered around the castle, ducking

in and out of rooms. She turned left down a long hallway, then veered right at a winding staircase. Eventually she found herself in the East Library, where she'd never been. Miranda liked how the dimming afternoon sunlight filled the room and how the books were arranged by color. Then her eyes stopped on a gleaming typewriter in front of a large window.

Miranda had never had any interest in writ-

ing before, but the typewriter was so lovely that she couldn't help walking over to it. *If only it were yellow*, she thought, *then it would make a great prop.* (Miranda's first decision as prop master had been that all the props for *Banana Pants* would be yellow.) Miranda wondered whether she should let Maude know about the typewriter, since she loved letter writing so much. *She's probably writing letters right now*, Miranda thought.

Ugh. She'd never understand why Maude wanted to spend so much time writing a letter about the leatherback turtle when turtles couldn't even read or understand that they were endangered.

Letters should be written to people who would be excited to read a letter, Miranda thought, putting her index finger on the shiny *W* key. Then she put her finger on the *K* key. Miranda could think of two people who would love to read a letter. Especially one that was written on such a beautiful typewriter. And hadn't Miss Kinde herself said, *"Sometimes ideas need to happen before others can see how good they are"*? Miranda looked around to make sure she was alone, and then she did an extremely unusual thing. She wrote two letters!

WHAT MIRANDA'S LETTERS SAID

Dear Miss Kinde,

I think you are a very kind person.
I hope you are free on the evening
of the world premiere of Banana
Pants. I would like to watch it with
you.
Sincerely,
A Secret Admirer

PS: After the play, we can share
some soup.

Dear Mr. Kaye,

I think you are a very nice person
with interesting quotes. I hope you
are free on the evening of the world
premiere of Banana Pants. I would
like to watch it with you. After the
play, we can have some soup.
Sincerely,

A Secret Admirer
PS: Your soup was delicious!

A SUPER-DUPER EXTRA-EARLY DELIVERY

Friday morning, Miranda woke up so early that QM and KD were still asleep. Quietly, she got dressed, ate breakfast, and went out to Blake, who was waiting to take her to school in the fancy royal automobile.

"You're early," Blake said. He didn't look up from his newspaper.

"Maude's house first," she whispered, climbing into the back of the car. "Then school."

If Blake wondered why Miranda was whispering, he didn't let on. He nodded, put down the newspaper, started the royal automobile, and drove to Maude's.

When Blake parked, Miranda took a shiny gold envelope out of her bag, opened the Kayes' mailbox, and put the envelope inside. Then she hopped back into the car and told Blake she was ready to go to school.

When Miranda arrived at 3B, Miss Kinde wasn't in the room, but Miranda knew Miss Kinde was at school, because a practice exam was already on her desk. Very quickly, Miranda took a second gold envelope out of her bag and placed it on her teacher's desk.

When Miss Kinde came into the room thirty seconds later, Miranda was sitting at her desk working on her exam.

14

MAUDE'S LATE-NIGHT LETTER WRITING

When Miranda slipped the love letter into Maude's mailbox that early morning, Maude wasn't sleeping. But Maude didn't see Miranda or hear the fancy automobile because she was busy writing her ninety-seventh letter. Or rather, the princess's ninety-seventh letter! After the excitement of the plastic lunch trays, Maude had spent the entire night writing.

Here are a few of the letters Maude had written:

Dear Mayor Lorraine,

Lemon Lake is very dirty. The town should clean it. If Lemon Lake was clean, the fish would come back and be happy. Families could swim there and be outside. My very best friend, Maude Brandywine Mayhew Kaye, would not have fished out a folding chair when she tried to fish there last summer.

Sincerely,

Princess Miranda
Rose Lapointsetta

Dear Fishmann Fisheries,

Please stop fishing in our beautiful lakes. You are taking all of the fish, which is very bad for underwater sea life. Underwater sea life is very important and affects birds and plants and people too!

Sincerely,

Princess Miranda
Rose Lapointsetta

Dear Panda Plastics,

Please stop polluting the air. Dirty air is not good for children, grown-ups, plants, or animals. Dirty air smells bad too. Who wants to smell bad-smelling air? Not me!

Sincerely,

Princess Miranda Rose Lapointsetta

But by the time Miranda had put her letter in the Kayes' mailbox, an exhausted Maude was writing a different kind of letter, like this one:

Dear Rainbow Sweeties Company,

I think you are the most delicious candy in the world! You are so small and shiny and sugary.
I love you! Please send me a bunch of Rainbow Sweeties for free!

Your best friend,

Princess Miranda
Rose Lapointsetta

15

BANANA PANTS REHEARSAL WITH DIRECTOR HILLARY GREENLIGHT-MILLER, TAKE ONE

After Maude's long night and Miranda's early morning, the girls were exhausted at Hillary Greenlight-Miller's first official day as *Banana Pants* director. Hillary, on the other hand, was very much awake and seized her directorial debut with a small megaphone and an

extremely long Things to Do List.

Hillary's first direction was to inform Donut that he would star in *Banana Pants*.

"I'm not the star," Donut

protested. "I'm craft services! I brought grapes and cheese for today."

"What kind of cheese?" Maude asked.

"No craft services," Hillary said. "We can't share food, Donut. Hello, rules twelve and thirteen!"

"Pick someone else for the lead," Donut said.

"Nope," replied Hillary. "Norbert already cast all the minor characters. Maude is the Onion. Miranda is the Mysterious Silent Woman with the Fish. Desdemona is the Game Show Host. Felix is Copernicus. We need a lead."

"I can't be the lead."

"Of course you can. It was *your* pants that got us here." Hillary checked something off the Things to Do List and exhaled. "Maude, in addition to being the Onion, you're fly crew. Okay?"

Maude yawned and nodded.

"Do you know what fly crew is?"

Maude shook her head. "But I like flying even more than I like onions. I mean, I think I'd like it. I like birds." She yawned again and rubbed her left hand, which was achy from her long night of letter writing. But she was determined to keep going! Maybe her next letter should be about saving the kakapo!

"Fly crew has nothing to do with birds." Hillary sounded exasperated. "Fly crew means you raise and lower the curtain. Here." She shoved a complicated diagram at Maude.

Maude glanced at the instructions. "Easy peasy."

"You'll do it?"

"Sure thing, boss," Maude replied.

"Props going well?" Hillary asked Miranda.

Miranda nodded happily. Miss Kinde must have read the love letter by now! And Walt could be reading his this very minute. All was going according to plan! "I brought dozens of yellow objects," she told Hillary. "And I can do a good job as the Mysterious Silent Woman with the Fish, too."

"Great!" Hillary stormed off to check on Agnes and Agatha and their mammoth roll of yellow felt.

"I don't want to be the lead," Donut whined when Hillary was gone. "Let's switch, Maude. I'd make an excellent onion."

"Sorry, Donut," Maude said. "I'm too busy to star in the show."

"This is a really dumb idea," Donut said miserably.

"Are you kidding?" Maude asked. "It's not

dumb. I am *thrilled* to be an onion and fly crew. More than that, I am *supremely thrilled* to not be taking another dumb practice exam."

"I love our creative endeavor," Agnes said, stitching an inseam. "I'm learning so much math from measuring all these pant legs."

"I was actually excited to come to school today," Felix added from behind a small mountain of wood. "I haven't been excited about school since . . . never!" He happily smashed his hammer onto a tiny nail. Bits of sawdust flew up into the room.

"*Banana Pants* isn't dumb," Miranda said firmly. She needed Donut to be the lead, because if he wasn't, then the play might not happen, and then Miss Kinde and Walt wouldn't watch it, and then they wouldn't eat soup afterward, and her cause wouldn't work!

"Don't worry, Donut," Maude said. "All it takes to be the lead is learning your lines and speaking loudly."

"Do you see how many lines Norbert is writing?" Donut pointed to Norbert, who appeared to

 be writing with both hands.

"And I can't speak loudly when I'm on a stage," Donut said loudly. "When I think about everyone looking at me, my mouth goes gluey." Donut sucked on his tongue. "Just talking about a stage makes me thirsty."

"Let's go to the auditorium," Miranda suggested. "I'll set up my props, Maude can practice raising and lowering the curtain, and Donut can—"

"DONUT CAN GET COMFORTABLE ON-STAGE," Hillary hollered into her megaphone, which was completely unnecessary since she was just four feet away.

"Wow," Maude said softly. "Our director is certainly giving lots of directions."

"I'M GOING TO IGNORE THAT, MAUDE," Hillary bellowed. "MIRANDA, THAT'S A GOOD IDEA. GET THEE TO THE STAGE!"

UNDER A RAINCOAT, UP ON A STAGE

As Donut, Maude, and Miranda walked to the auditorium, Donut imagined running out of school, past the big tree by the entrance, and all the way home, where, without stopping, he'd tell his mom he loved her. Then he'd run until he was so far from Mountain River Valley Elementary that Hillary would have to find another lead. While Donut pictured his escape, Miranda wished that her letters had told Miss Kinde and Walt where to sit during the play. What if they ended up on opposite sides of the auditorium? Maude was thinking about all the letters she'd write once the curtain was raised. Since her part as the onion wasn't until act three, she'd have a lot of free time once the play started.

When they walked into the auditorium, the three students looked around. The curtain was neither up nor down. The stage seemed enormous and empty. And there were so very many seats! Would they really be able to pull off their creative endeavor?

"Come on, Donut," Miranda urged. "Get onstage."

Slowly, Donut walked to the stage. Trembling, he hoisted himself onto it. Then he stood there.

"Do something," Maude said.

"Like what?" Donut said quietly.

"Anything," Miranda said encouragingly.

Donut licked his lips. "I'm thirsty," he whispered.

"Imagine you're drinking water," Maude told him. "Like a mime."

Donut didn't move.

"Sing the banana song," Miranda suggested.

Donut said something so quietly, the girls couldn't hear him.

The girls looked at each other. Donut put his head in his hands.

After a long silence, Maude said, "Well, I'm going to see about raising this curtain."

While Maude went into the wings, Miranda lugged a bag of props onto the stage. She took out an enormous neon-yellow raincoat, a yellow abacus, a brass lamp with a mustard-yellow shade, two ceramic vases with yellow daisies in them, and a valuable painting of a lemon. When she finished arranging them, she looked out into the empty seats. In no time, it would be show-time, and because of her love letters, Miss Kinde and Walt would find each other! If the play and the soup went well, then maybe, not too far in the future, Miss Kinde and Walt would ask Miranda to be the prop master for their wedding! At the wedding, Maude would come up to Miranda and say, "Thank you for believing in love! This wonderful day wouldn't have happened without you. Love *is* a cause, and because of you, I love love!"

"Holy bananas!" Maude hollered from the wings.

Miranda left her daydream and returned to the grimy stage. "What's wrong?" she called.

"The curtain is really heavy!" Maude yelled back.

Miranda got up and walked over to Maude, who was pulling on the curtain rope with all her might.

"You're doing it right?" Miranda asked nervously. If Maude couldn't raise the curtain, how could 3B perform their play?

Maude nodded. "You try."

Miranda pulled on the ancient rope. Nothing happened. She tugged a little harder. Still nothing. *How can this be?* she wondered in a panic.

"It's stuck," Maude said. "Stuck, stuck, stuck."

"Like me," said a very quiet voice.

Miranda and Maude peeked out from behind the curtain. There was Donut, hiding under the enormous yellow raincoat in a dusty corner of the stage.

17

MAUDE SAYS NO

After the first *Banana Pants* rehearsal, Maude climbed up the twenty-seven slightly crooked stairs into her house. "Hello!" she shouted.

"Greetings," said Walt, who was in a backbend. "How's the creative endeavor going?"

"Well, we're certainly endeavoring," she said. "My onion-ing is top-notch of course. Unfortunately, Norbert wrote so much today that I'm not actually an onion until act four." Maude scrunched her face in thought. "Or maybe it's act five."

"Whatever the act, you'll make a terrific onion," Walt said.

"The only problem is that

the curtain I have to raise is actually pretty heavy."

"Theater curtains can be tricky," Walt said.

"Other than that, I'm sure *Banana Pants* will be . . ." *How will it be?* Maude wondered. In addition to the heavy curtain, Donut had nearly fainted when he saw how many lines Norbert had written for him. He'd recovered from that only to nearly faint again when he saw the extremely tight yellow pants Agatha and Agnes had sewed. Plus, Felix's sets were getting enormous, Fletcher didn't seem to understand that he was the best dancer in the class, and Desdemona thought everyone knew how to cartwheel. Luckily for Maude, the onion didn't dance or sing or cartwheel.

"Once I get the curtain raised, my parts should be okay," Maude told Walt. She felt extremely relieved that *Banana Pants* was Hillary's problem, since she had much more important things to think about, like which companies the princess should write to next.

Walt flipped, stood up, and picked up a gold

envelope from the table. "Look what I got in the mail today."

"*You* got a letter?" Maude asked.

Walt nodded and held it out. "Read it."

Maude read the letter. For a moment, she wondered if, in her late-night letter-writing craze, she'd accidentally written the letter to her dad. But that was bananas! This was not the kind of letter Maude would write. She wrote important letters! But she knew, without a doubt, who *would* write this kind of letter. Not only did it sound like a certain princess who lived one point two miles away, but there was also a tiny crown on the bottom of the page. Only one family in town had stationery like that!

"I don't think who you think wrote that letter wrote it," Maude told her dad. "It was definitely, without a doubt, *not* Miss Kinde. I know that one hundred percent. For a fact."

Walt smiled. "I don't care who wrote it. I'm just excited to see the play. What do you think about having a cast party here?"

"Cast party?" Maude asked, but really she was

thinking, *How could Miranda write that letter? How could she do such a thing?*

"It's customary to have a party after a show," Walt said. "Let's have it here. We still have plenty of soup. Everyone could come!"

"Everyone?" Maude asked. "Miss Kinde?"

"Sure. Miss Kinde, the whole cast and crew of *Banana Pants*, Principal Fish, Miranda's parents, Donut's mom, everyone!"

"No," Maude said. "I don't want anyone eating soup here."

"Oh," Walt said sadly. "It might be nice . . ."

"No cast party," she said firmly.

"All right," Walt said. "But if you change your mind, you know where to find me." He picked up a book called *Everything You Wanted to Know About Beetles but Were Afraid to Ask*. "I'll be in my office if you need me," he said.

"Maybe you should change your mind," Michael-John said.

Maude jumped. She hadn't even noticed her brother was sitting on the couch, surrounded by books and sleeping pets.

"About the cast party?" she asked. Not only was she surprised that she hadn't seen him, she was more surprised that he had an opinion about cast parties.

Michael-John nodded.

"I don't want Miss Kinde eating soup here!" Maude stomped her foot, which startled Rosalie and Onion the Great Number Eleven awake. Rudolph Valentino kept sleeping.

"It wouldn't be just Miss Kinde. Dad said everybody would be invited. Anyway, I thought you liked Miss Kinde."

"I love Miss Kinde. But . . ." How could Maude explain any of this to her brother?

"I think it might be good for us to have a party

here, Maude. It's been a long time," Michael-
John said.

It was true. Before Maude and Michael-John's
mom died, they'd had loads of parties: soup parties, dance parties, turn-out-the-lights-and-
sing-as-loud-as-you-can parties.

"Dad needs friends," Michael-John said.

"Dad has friends," Maude said, although she
wasn't so sure. She'd never really thought about
it.

"Dad *knows* a lot of people," Michael-John
said. "The beetle experts, all the yogis, the quo-
tation society. But those people aren't really
friends. You know what a real friend is."

Maude looked at the secret-admirer letter on
the table. "Friends are overrated," she said.

"Friends are extremely important," Michael-
John said.

"Do *you* have friends?" Maude asked her
brother, even though she knew he didn't because
he just stayed home in pajamas reading dictionaries all day. Although, actually, he wasn't in
pajamas now.

Michael-John's eyes grew wide. "Of course I have friends! I have tons of friends, Maude."

"Oh," Maude said.

"Wait—do you think I just stay home in my pajamas reading dictionaries all day?"

Maude was shocked. "Uh, um, well . . . Who are your friends? When do you see them?"

"My friends are other students who choose to do school at home," Michael-John said. "I see them Mondays, Wednesdays, and Fridays. And the occasional Tuesday afternoon."

Stunned, Maude put her glasses on. *How could I not know this?* she wondered. Then again, when was the last time she'd asked her brother what he'd done while she was at school? Normally, she burst into the house, announced what she'd done that day, and had a snack. Today she hadn't even noticed him! And he was right there.

"Just today, I met up with Gwyneth-Rose, Sarah-Rose, Sadie, Jedidiah, Rachel-Jane, and Fred," Michael-John continued. "We went to the museum and rode mountain bikes."

"Oh." Maude put her glasses back on top of her head and stroked her chicken.

"I know you have perfect vision," Michael-John said. "But once in a while, maybe you should look up from your letter writing and see what other people are doing. You might be surprised."

"I see plenty of things," Maude said quietly.

But Michael-John had gone back to reading his comic book and didn't seem to hear her.

18

THE FIGHT

Early Monday morning, Maude met Miranda at the entrance of Mountain River Valley Elementary.

"Maude! Is waking up early your new cause?" Miranda laughed. "I don't think Miss Kinde is going to let you in again."

"I'm not going in," Maude said. She was wearing her favorite bandana, her VOTES FOR WOMEN sash, and a shirt that said SAVE THE SAOLA with a picture of a small, two-horned animal underneath. "I got up early because of this." She held out Walt's letter, which she'd secretly swiped.

Miranda nodded slowly. For some reason, in all her daydreaming about Miss Kinde and Walt, she'd never imagined Maude reading the letter.

"I know you wrote this," Maude said. "Now my dad wants to have a cast party at my house and it's all your fault."

"But a cast party at your house is a great idea," Miranda said. "Miss Kinde would love that. She hasn't said anything about her letter yet, but . . ."

"You wrote Miss Kinde a letter, too?"

"Well, yes," Miranda said. "I couldn't just write one love letter. There had to be two!"

Maude scowled. "How could you? There are so many better things to write about than stupid love!"

"Just because I don't want to write about Styrofoam or mountain gorillas doesn't mean love is stupid," Miranda said.

"But Styrofoam and mountain gorillas are important!" Maude shouted. "Love is not important. Love is silly!"

"It is not," Miranda said, getting mad. "Love *is* important, Maude. Love makes people happy! Don't you want people to be happy? You've never seen a saola. Why do you want to spend your time trying to save something you've never even seen?"

"If I don't try to save the saola, who will?" Maude asked. "I can't believe you won't think about the big, wide world."

"The small world is important, too," Miranda said. "Love is a cause, too. Miss Kinde said so! That's the whole reason for the creative endeavor. To spend time doing something we love! Just because my cause isn't about something endangered or polluted doesn't mean it's not important!"

"I hate love!" Maude shrieked. "And I hate you for writing stupid love letters." And with that,

Maude stormed off, leaving Miranda alone at the door.

19

EVEN WORSE WITHOUT A FRIEND

The week of the fight was fabulous for everyone except for Donut, who was very, very nervous, and for Miranda and Maude, who were too angry to enjoy the last week of their creative endeavor.

On Tuesday, Hillary added four hundred more things to her Things to Do List. On Wednesday, Fletcher introduced a thunderclap, a reverse turn, and a feather step to his dance routines. On Thursday, Desdemona perfected her front hand-spring and her back walkover.

Norbert wrote three new acts three days in a row!

"I have too many lines," Donut told him on Friday morning. "Can't you make *Banana Pants* shorter?"

"No," Norbert said firmly. "Every single word is important!"

Agatha had spent most of the week sewing yellow buttons onto a pair of yellow pants.

But Agnes preferred gold buttons to yellow, and she had sewn hers onto the spaces Agatha had missed.

"Those pants look heavy," Donut told them. "How many buttons are on those pants anyway?"

Agnes did some quick math. "Nine hundred," she said.

"And the left leg looks longer than the right."

"Agnes did that side," Agatha said.

"Did not," Agnes said, sewing on another gold button.

Felix had constructed a mountain of planks so high and wide it blocked nearly half of the stage.

"Your sets are so big, no one can see my props," Miranda told him quietly. But she didn't care about her props anymore, now that she and Maude weren't talking. She glanced over at Maude, who was onstage in front of the curtain she still hadn't been able to raise, being an onion. Or maybe she was garlic.

Curled up on the dusty stage, Maude couldn't remember if she was an onion or a clove of garlic, since Norbert had given her several additional minor roles. She didn't care about creative endeavors anymore.

But when they weren't working on *Banana Pants*, school was even worse for Miranda and Maude that week.

They both got bonked on the head during gym class because, for the first time in their friendship, they were on opposite sides of the net and couldn't yell "duck" when Coach Corsica hurled balls at them. Then they both got horrible headaches during music class because hearing their classmates play their recorders was unbearable without some-one to complain to about how unbearable it was.

Lunch for both girls was especially miserable on Friday. Miranda sat on the left side of the table. Maude sat on the right, slowly eating soup and trying not to look at Miranda's enormous, most-likely delicious lunch. Staring into her bottomless container of soup, Maude wondered if a cast party would have been a good idea, if only to make a dent in the never-ending soup situation. She also tried not to think about her brother out with all his friends while her dad was home alone with his already-discovered beetle. *What had Michael-John meant about looking up? I see plenty of people. Don't I?* Right now, she could see Miranda happily enjoying her enormous, delicious lunch with Felix and Norris.

But Miranda was not enjoying her enormous, delicious lunch. Sitting next to Felix and Norris was not nearly as much fun as sitting with Maude. She didn't laugh once, and she had so much lunch left, since Felix and Norris, unlike Maude, wouldn't break any food-sharing rules. Miranda got up from the table and walked over to the back of the cafeteria. There was a lot less garbage there, now that the trash cans weren't piled up with Styrofoam trays. *Maude is probably happy to see this*, Miranda thought. *But it's too bad there isn't a better place to put this food*, she thought as she dumped her leftover lunch. *At the castle and at Maude's house, there's a compost bin*, she thought, walking back to the table. *Why can't there be a compost bin at Mountain River Valley?* Miranda's heart jolted. She'd thought of another cause! Should she tell Maude? *No*, she thought. She'd never tell, because Maude thought all of her causes were better! And anyway, Miranda reminded herself, they were in a fight!

20

AN EXTREMELY
TERRIBLE WEEKEND

For 3B, the weekend before the performance of *Banana Pants* was terrible. Norbert tried to make his script shorter but cried every time he erased a word. He loved them all too much! Hillary found that she could only *add* things to her Things to Do List, and Felix glued so much wood together that he accidentally barricaded himself in his room. Donut tried to book a trip out of the country, but his mom kept stopping him and making him practice his (zillions of) lines. Desdemona broke her grandmother's favorite lamp trying to learn Fletcher's still-impossible dance routines.

Since Felix's sets were too big for anyone to see her props, Miranda moped around the castle looking for something to do. She avoided the East Library with the beautiful typewriter, but even in the fun rooms (indoor trampoline! rope swings!), she was bored and grumpy. Eventually, she found herself in the kitchen, where Blake was frosting tiny cupcakes.

"Blake? What are you doing down here?" Miranda was surprised. She couldn't remember the last time she'd seen Blake anywhere but in the car.

Blake didn't look up. "I could ask the same of you."

"I'm . . . I don't know."

"Oh. Well, as you can see, I'm frosting tiny cupcakes."

"Why?"

"I don't just drive, you know. I wanted to do something different today. Something challenging."

"Is Chef Blue driving?" Miranda asked curiously.

Blake shook his head. "Absolutely not! He doesn't have a license."

"Oh."

"Are you all right?" Blake asked. "You seem . . ." He looked up from the tiny cupcake he was frosting.

"I'm fine," Miranda said. And then she promptly burst into tears.

After she stopped crying, Miranda told Blake everything about Maude's causes and her love cause and *Banana Pants*, and how the beautiful typewriter in the East Library had made her realize she could write secret love letters.

"Secret love letters?" Blake asked.

"I wrote two letters. One to Miss Kinde and

one to Walt. They were about watching *Banana Pants* together and eating soup."

Blake nodded.

"They both like soup and theater. There could have been a cast party at Maude's after the play. I thought if Maude could see how happy Miss Kinde and Walt were, she'd realize I was right about my love cause."

Blake nodded again.

"Remember the early morning when you drove me to Maude's?"

"I do."

"I was putting the letter in Maude's mailbox."

Blake nodded a third time and handed Miranda a tiny cupcake, which she began to frost, even though she didn't like cupcakes or frosting.

Blake's tiny cupcakes were lovely shades of green and blue, but Miranda's cupcake turned out yellow—banana yellow—which made her think about the play and that early morning two weeks ago, before she'd even heard of a creative endeavor. Suddenly, Miranda remembered Maude saying, *"Don't get my dad into any love cause or anything. Okay?"*

And she had said okay! She'd agreed! But she wrote those letters anyway!

The princess made a dreadful noise.

Blake looked up.

"Maude asked me not to do something and I did it anyway," Miranda told him.

Blake looked at Miranda. "It might be wonderful if Walt and Miss Kinde ate soup at a cast party. I think the world would be a better place if more people came together to eat soup."

Miranda's eyes grew wide. Blake understood! He believed love was a cause! She wasn't wrong!

"But," Blake said, "Maude told you not to get involved and you did it anyway. You went against her wishes for *your* own reasons. That's wrong, no matter how good your intentions were."

Miranda blinked back hot tears. "I wish I'd never found that stupid beautiful typewriter! Then I never would've written those stupid secret love letters!"

Blake looked at Miranda thoughtfully before he said, "But typewriters don't write secret love letters. *People* write secret love letters."

"What do I do now?" Miranda asked.

"Apologize," Blake said matter-of-factly.

"Apologize?" Miranda said the word like she'd never heard it before. "How?"

Blake smiled as he frosted his last tiny cupcake. "If you can figure out what to say in two secret love letters," he said, "I'm certain you can figure out how to say you're sorry."

21

OVER IN THE KAYES' KITCHEN

While Miranda was crying over Blake's tiny cupcakes, Maude was in her kitchen staring at Michael-John, who had just screeched, "Enough!," put down his dictionary, ran outside, gathered chicken eggs, and brought them into the house.

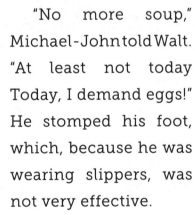

"No more soup," Michael-John told Walt. "At least not today Today, I demand eggs!" He stomped his foot, which, because he was wearing slippers, was not very effective.

Maude and Walt stared at Michael-John. "All right," Walt said, putting a frying pan on the stove.

"Wow," Maude said to her brother. "That was . . ." *What was it?* It definitely wasn't like Michael-John.

"That was something *you'd* do," Michael-John said, putting slices of bread into the toaster. "I was sitting on the couch, dreading another soupy meal. I looked at you and thought that if Maude wanted to stop Dad from serving more soup, she'd do something loud and sudden. That's not what I would do, but then I thought, why not? What's the worst that can happen? And now look!" Michael-John said happily. "Eggs and toast!"

Hmmmm, Maude thought. If Michael-John did something like her and it worked, maybe she should try doing something like him. After all, she wasn't having much luck doing things like herself lately. Michael-John had loads of friends, and without Miranda, Maude was just a lonely onion (or was it garlic?) who was too weak to raise (or lower) a theater curtain. Waiting for her eggs, Maude opened a dictionary. She flipped through it, not paying attention, until a word jumped out:

Forgery: noun: the crime of falsely making or changing a written paper or signing someone else's name.

Maude read the entry again. *Forgery?*

"Is a letter 'a written paper'?" she asked, even though she knew the answer.

"Absolutely," Walt said, putting a steaming plate of scrambled eggs in front of her. "The writer Lewis Carroll once said, 'The proper definition of a man is an animal that writes letters.'"

Maude took a bite of egg, closed the dictionary, and put her head on top of it. She'd signed "Princess Miranda Rose Lapointsetta" so many times she'd probably forgotten how to sign her own name! She felt sick. Was something wrong with the eggs Walt had just made? Or was it that she, Maude Brandywine Mayhew Kaye, social justice activist extraordinaire, was a criminal!

22

THE DRESS REHEARSAL

Monday morning, an exhausted 3B walked into the auditorium. They looked around at the empty seats, the stage with the curtain that was neither up nor down, and the enormous sets that still needed to be lifted onto the stage. It seemed impossible that, in just ten hours, there'd be an actual audience!

"OKAY, PEOPLE!" Hillary Greenlight-Miller hollered into her megaphone. "THIS IS OUR ONE AND ONLY DRESS REHEARSAL. FIND YOUR PLACES!" She clutched her Things to Do List.

Slowly, Donut walked to the front of the stage, opened his mouth, and said . . . absolutely nothing.

"DONUT!" Hillary bellowed.

"I can't do it," Donut whispered. "The play is still too long, the dances are still too hard, the

107

pants have way too many buttons and are still much too tight."

Hillary looked around. "DIDN'T ANYONE MAKE ANY CHANGES THIS WEEKEND? I GAVE *LOTS* OF DIRECTIONS."

"The play is *not* too long," Norbert said. "It's perfect."

"I have fifty-five lines, Norbert," Agnes said. "And I'm not even a lead."

"My dances aren't too hard," Fletcher said. "Everyone should practice."

"We've been practicing," Agatha and Desdemona whined.

The class looked at Donut's pants, but it was impossible to deny their tightness and the ridiculous number of gold and yellow buttons.

"Yellow buttons are stylish," Agatha mumbled.

"Gold ones are better," Agnes said.

"And what's going on with the curtain?" Norris asked.

3B looked at Maude and then at one another with almost as much dread as they felt before taking a practice exam. If they didn't do something,

Banana Pants would be a disaster, and Principal Fish would never let another class have a creative endeavor.

Hillary Greenlight-Miller looked at her cast and crew and tried to remember what things had been like before *Banana Pants*, back when 3B was just 3B. Hillary thought about that long-ago Monday morning when Desdemona happily shared about her gymnastics show and Donut talked about his French crullers, and Agnes and Agatha, the very best of friends, were thrilled with their simple, tiny animal clothes.

And then something unexpected happened.

Hillary Greenlight-Miller put her megaphone down. She walked down the aisle, got on the stage, and walked over to Donut, who was trembling. The class held their breath, but Hillary did not yell. She did not say anything as she very dramatically tore up her Things to Do List.

3B gasped.

"What are you doing?" Norbert asked, his voice cracking. "That list was so long! There were so many words."

Hillary looked out at the class. "I," she said loudly, "am endeavoring."

No one said anything.

"Remember when we first learned what a creative endeavor was?"

The class nodded.

"Our purpose was to put on a class play, right?" Hillary asked.

"Right," Norbert and Fletcher and Desdemona said.

"Well," Hillary continued, "the playwright George Bernard Shaw said that 'the quality of a play is the quality of its ideas.'"

"Wow," Maude said quietly. "That's something my dad would quote!"

"I think our idea, *Banana Pants*, is of good quality."

"Thank you," Norbert said.

Hillary shook her head. "But we took our own ideas too far." She picked up a handful of the torn-up list and threw it in the air. "And I put too many things on this list," she said. "I forgot about the people—the people who had the good ideas for the play."

3B nodded.

"Donut," Hillary said almost gently. "Close your eyes."

"What?"

"Trust me," Hillary said.

Donut closed his eyes.

"Now, imagine that the audience isn't people. Imagine that the audience is doughnuts."

"Doughnuts?" 3B said.

"Doughnuts," Hillary repeated. "Imagine chocolate doughnuts, jelly doughnuts, coco-nut doughnuts, delicious rainbow-sprinkled doughnuts."

Donut imagined hundreds of doughnuts

eagerly waiting to hear what he had to stay. *I could be king of the doughnuts*, he thought. His mouth started to water, and his tongue got unglued from the roof of his mouth.

"Once upon a dark and stormy night," Donut said loudly and clearly. "There was a pair of extremely yellow pants."

3B cheered. If Hillary could put down her megaphone and rip up her list, and Donut could say the opening lines, there was nothing they couldn't do. Right away, Norbert cut the entire first act. Although he shed a tear here and there, he had to admit that, without act one, the actors could learn all of their lines and there was much less of a chance that the audience would fall asleep. Inspired by Norbert's willingness to cut his words, Fletcher simplified his dance numbers and agreed that Desdemona could do a front handspring at the end of each one. By lunch, Agnes and Agatha had doubled the width and length of Donut's pants and removed almost all of the buttons, and Felix had sawed his mountainous sets in two so the stage was visible.

Now that Miranda was able to put her props in the correct places on the more reasonably sized sets, and her already small role of Silent Mysterious Woman with the Fish was even smaller, she had only one thing left to do. Which was the hardest thing of all. Taking a deep breath, she walked behind the stage and over to Maude, who was still trying to raise the curtain. Miranda's heart began to race, and she felt as thirsty as Donut had been on the stage. Apologizing to Maude seemed impossible!

But then she remembered what Maude had said that first early morning. Miranda could clearly hear Maude saying, *"It's* not *impossible! When you do something wrong, you apologize. You say, 'Sorry, that was a terrible idea. I won't do it ever again'!"*

"Maude," Miranda said, her heart thumping wildly, "I am sorry. My secret letter writing was a terrible idea."

Maude let go of the curtain rope and turned to look at her friend.

"I won't do it ever again," Miranda said. "You asked me not to and I did it anyway. That was wrong."

Maude smiled. "I didn't want you to write love letters," she said. "But I think . . . I think it might be good for my dad to make friends. You were right about that." She shrugged. "Love is not my cause. But it doesn't mean it can't be yours. But no more secret love letters," she added.

"Never," Miranda said, full of relief. "I promise. I don't want to write any more letters. At least not on my own. But I did think of another cause."

Maude gave Miranda a doubtful look.

"Composting!" Miranda squealed. "Shouldn't Mountain River Valley compost?"

Maude's eyes grew wide. How had she never thought of that? Composting was a terrifically amazing idea!

"I thought of it when I was throwing out my lunch," Miranda explained. "Now that the

Styrofoam trays are gone, there's less garbage. But there could be *even less* if Mountain River Valley composted the leftover food."

"Wow," Maude said.

"Speaking of food, or rather candy, this came for me the other day. I have no idea why." Miranda held out a packet of Rainbow Sweeties.

Maude stared at the candy.

"There are five big boxes of them at the castle, too. I don't know why I'm getting so much candy. I thought everyone knew I don't like sweets."

Miranda pushed the packet closer to Maude, but Maude didn't take them.

"Is it because of rule sixty-eight?" Miranda asked. Rule sixty-eight stated that candy could not be eaten in school unless it was a national holiday. This made no sense, since school was never open on national holidays.

Maude shook her head.

"Are you still mad?" Miranda sounded worried.

Maude shook her head again.

"But you love candy. And Rainbow Sweeties are your absolute favorite."

"That candy is part of my heinous crime!" Maude shouted, dashing out from behind the curtain and across the stage just as Donut, Desdemona, and Agnes were finally getting the hang of Fletcher's easier version of the jitterbug.

23

FORGIVENESS IN A TREE

Without thinking about all the rules she was breaking, Miranda followed Maude across the stage, down the hallway, and over to the trunk of Maude's favorite tree in front of the school.

"Don't come up," Maude called to Miranda through her tears.

"Why not?" Miranda yelled.

"You're afraid of heights."

Miranda nodded. She *was* afraid of heights, but if she could apologize, then she could climb a tree! Holding her breath, Miranda hoisted herself up to the first branch. And then she stopped. Maude was several branches up, but Miranda wasn't going any higher. She also wasn't going to look down.

"You committed a crime?" She gazed up at Maude, who was staring at her hands.

Maude nodded glumly. "Forgery. It's a

noun and a crime. It means to fake. I forged a signature."

"Whose signature did you forge?"

Maude wiped her tears with a bright yellow bandana. "Yours."

"Mine?"

"I signed your name on the letter I wrote for the recyclable lunch trays. I snuck the letter into Principal Fish's office."

"And it worked."

Maude nodded sadly.

"But aren't you happy that the Styrofoam is gone? You've been writing those letters forever."

"I'd be happier if I'd signed my own name," Maude said. "And who knows if it was because of the forged letter. Maybe the trays just arrived that day. I'll never know."

"One letter isn't that bad," Miranda said generously.

Maude groaned. "It wasn't one letter. I got so excited by the lunch trays that I wrote . . ." She took a deep breath. "I forged your name on ninety-seven letters."

Miranda was quiet.

"And some of those letters weren't even for good causes . . . the Rainbow Sweeties . . ."

It didn't take long for Miranda to figure out what Maude had done. She thought about this for a minute. It was weird to think that her name was on so many letters!

"Are you mad?" Maude asked.

Am I mad? Miranda wondered. Maude had taken something from her—her beautiful name—without her permission! Ninety-seven times!

"Yes," Miranda said. "I'm mad."

"You have every right to be," Maude said. "I'll really miss you."

"Where are you going?"

Maude clenched her bandana to her heart. "Nowhere, but we can't be friends anymore . . . not after what I've done."

Miranda's heart jolted. Not be friends? That would be worse than forgery! And definitely not what she wanted.

"I'm mad you forged my name," Miranda

yelled. "But I still want to be friends. Don't friends forgive each other?"

Maude nodded. "I think so."

Miranda shifted slightly, making sure she didn't look down. "You won't forge again?"

"Never ever!" Maude scrambled down the tree branch. She sat next to Miranda and looked right in her eyes. "I am so sorry. Forging your name was a terrible idea. I won't do it ever again."

The girls looked at each other. They felt different. Their friendship felt different. A little bit bruised, but also a little bit stronger.

After a while, Maude said, "Who knew that Hillary would turn out to be such a good director? Letting her direct was one of my best ideas ever."

"Speaking of directing, do you want me to join fly crew?" Miranda asked. "I can help you lift up the curtain."

"You'd do that?"

Miranda nodded. "After the play is over, do you want to see the typewriter I found? We can type the compost letter."

"Let's do that tomorrow," Maude said. "Do you think it's too late to have a cast party at my house? I'll invite everyone. That way, my dad will have lots of people to talk to. And we might even run out of soup!"

"I don't think you're ever going to run out of soup," Miranda said sympathetically.

The girls looked at each other and laughed, until Hillary Greenlight-Miller ran out of the school looking for them. She didn't have her megaphone, but she was definitely yelling.

24

THE WORLD PREMIERE OF BANANA PANTS

Tickets for the world premiere of *Banana Pants*, which were free, sold out in record time. Despite the suggestion from their director that they remain unseen, 3B couldn't stop peeking out from behind the stage curtain, which was finally raised and then lowered, thanks to Miranda and Maude's combined strength. In the audience were all the students and teachers of Mountain River Valley Elementary. Principal Fish was in a center seat, clutching not only the *Official Rules of Mountain River Valley Elementary*, but also another book called *Official Rules for Elementary Theater*. Donut looked at his mom several times. He was very happy to see her, but he was mostly checking on the boxes next to her.

There were five big boxes of Rainbow Sweeties from Miranda, a large container of tiny cupcakes from an anonymous supporter of the arts, and an enormous box of doughnuts that Hillary had bought with her own money. Everything was going to Maude's house for the cast party after the show, but secretly Donut planned to eat most of the doughnuts himself.

Maude and Miranda were happy to spot their families in the crowd. QM and KD were there, along with Blake and Chef Blue. Walt was next to Michael-John, who was next to a group of kids who didn't go to Mountain River Valley. Rosalie, in Michael-John's lap, was making herself as small as possible, since chickens were not allowed in school. For one second, Miranda imagined Walt moving closer to Miss Kinde, but she threw that idea right out!

Which was kind of what had happened to Miss Kinde's letter. The girls didn't know it, but Miss Kinde had never even seen her secret love letter. Despite

Miranda's perfect placement, it had gotten mixed up in a bunch of old practice exams and was, at that very moment, getting shredded at a recycling center far, far away.

Just before showtime, Miss Kinde, in a fashionable banana sweater, strolled behind the curtain and gathered 3B around her. "No matter what happens tonight, I am extremely proud of you," she said. "You worked very hard on the ideas you were passionate about."

She smiled. "But I am most proud of the ways you came together."

3B nodded. They'd endeavored! All together!

"Are we ready?" Miss Kinde asked.

3B looked at one another nervously. But then Hillary smiled at Donut, who beamed at Fletcher, who smiled at Desdemona, who beamed at Agatha, who smiled at Agnes, who grinned at Norris, who smiled at Norbert, who beamed at Miranda, who grinned at Felix, who smiled at Maude, who actually grinned at Hillary. The truth was, 3B knew they weren't really ready. Who could put on a play in two weeks? But as someone once said, "The show must go on," and there wasn't any more time. The audience was waiting.

"We're ready, Miss Kinde," Hillary Greenlight-Miller said, with more confidence than she probably had. "Places, everyone."

Taking a deep breath and imaging all the doughnuts in his future, Donut walked to the center of the stage, his yellow pants billowing around him. The rest of 3B scurried to their spots.

Hillary looked at Maude and Miranda. "Fly crew: Curtain!"

Maude and Miranda saluted Hillary, looked

at each other, and together, putting one hand over the other and pulling with all their might, Princess Miranda Rose Lapointsetta and absolutely not a princess Maude Brandywine Mayhew Kaye raised Mountain River Valley Elementary's curtain high above the stage.

Perched on a rafter in the back of the auditorium, Norris shone a spotlight on Donut as Maude and Miranda secured the curtain.

"Break a leg!" Hillary Greenlight-Miller whispered. "But not really," she added, crossing her fingers as tightly as she could.

Maude and Miranda clasped their hands together, smiled at each other, and waited for *Banana Pants* to begin.

ACKNOWLEDGMENTS

I am fortunate to have an amazing crew that helped with this book. Thanks to Rachel Orr at the Prospect Agency, who has defended my writer rights for years.

Thanks to everyone at Abrams, especially Siobhán Gallagher, Andrew Smith, Jody Mosley, Evangelos Vasilakis, Erin Vandeveer, Nicole Schaefer, Patricia McNamara, Jenny Choy, Elisa Gonzalez, Rebecca Schmidt, Mary Wowk, and Michael Jacobs. An especially loud and clear thank you to Erica Finkel, editor extraordinaire, who brilliantly directed me to cut act one in this book. Thank her if you didn't fall asleep while reading.

I am grateful to superstar illustrator Jessika von Innerebner, who made Miranda and Maude (and the whole 3B world) come alive.

Thanks to the Mountain River Valley Writing Group. This isn't actually our name (yet), but everyone in it has an excellent sense of humor and I look forward to hearing all the words you think I should've cut from these acknowledgments.

Thanks to Claudia Palmer, who is so great to work with that she'd make taking a Mandatory National Reading and Writing and Math exam almost fun! I'm very grateful that my aunts Sarah and Chris generously let me write (and rewrite!) this book in the Vermont house.

Love to my parents and my brother, Jake, who are so encouraging and supportive, they'll probably each buy ninety-seven copies of this book!

A megaphone THANK YOU to Sadie Mielcarz, who read the first Miranda and Maude book nine hundred years ago. A gigantic thank you to Gwyn McGee, who was the first person not related to me to read this one. Sadie and Gwyn's interest and suggestions were totally worth the payment of pancakes (with tons of syrup) and one (gigantic) brownie sundae.

My husband, Nicholas Gaffney, is a thoughtful

listener, offers good advice, and was (mostly) understanding about the writing stretch when I protested the entire concept of laundry.

Georgia and Dahlia, my daughters, are the heart of Miranda and Maude. Their enthusiasm, along with the occasional reading over my shoulder (as I typed!), made the hard parts worth it.

Mostly, I feel fortunate that I had two Miss Kindes when I was in school. Mrs. Schweitzer (third grade) and Ms. Martha Weisberg (high school English) paved the way for me to become a writer by making me feel that my creative endeavors could be important. To all the Miss Kindes, who tirelessly support kids and their (sometimes) banana-pants projects, THANK YOU!

EMMA WUNSCH

Emma Wunsch's theater career began and ended with her role as Kangaroo in a town production of *Peter Pan*. It was a non-speaking part, which might be why she became a writer. *Banana Pants!* is her second chapter book in the Miranda and Maude series. She lives in Lebanon, New Hampshire, with her husband and their two daughters.

JESSIKA VON INNEREBNER

Jessika von Innerebner is an artist who's worked with clients including Disney, Nickelodeon, *Highlights*, and Fisher-Price. She lives in Kelowna, Canada.

**VISIT HER ONLINE AT
JESSVONI.COM**

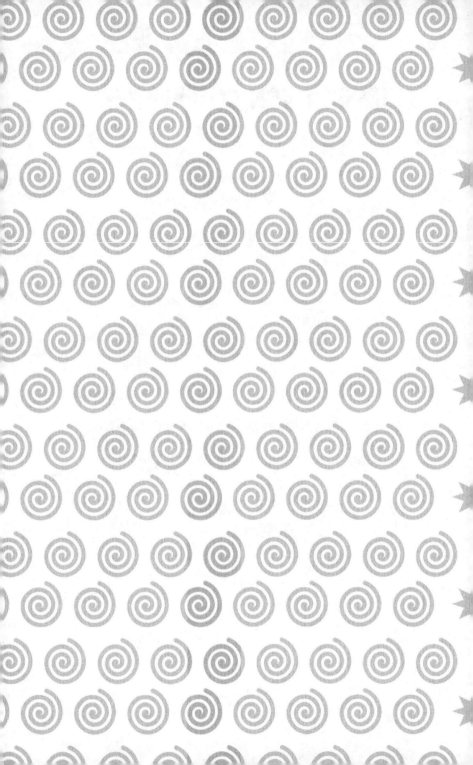